one summer
UP NORTH

john owens

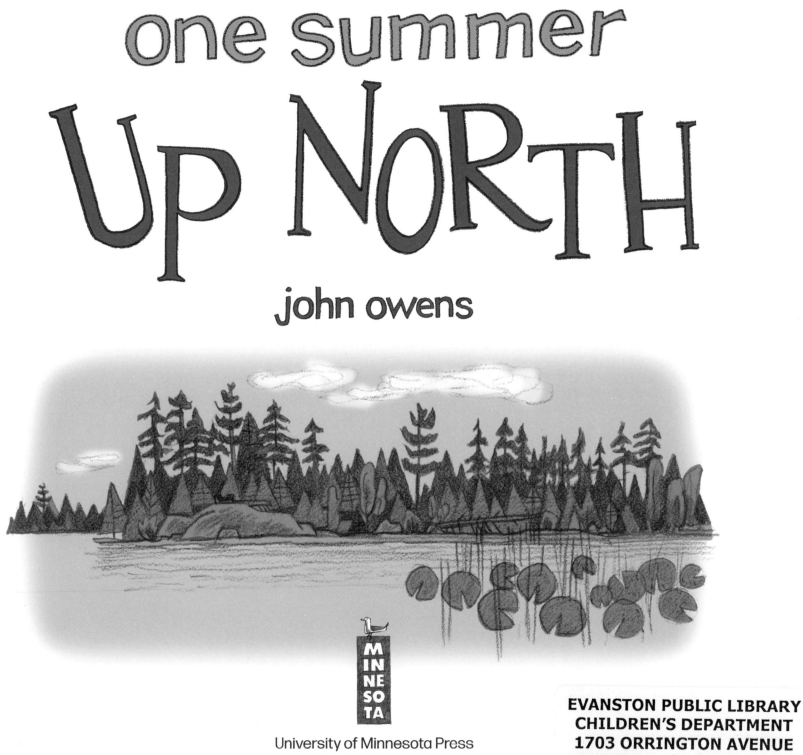

MINNESOTA

University of Minnesota Press
Minneapolis | London

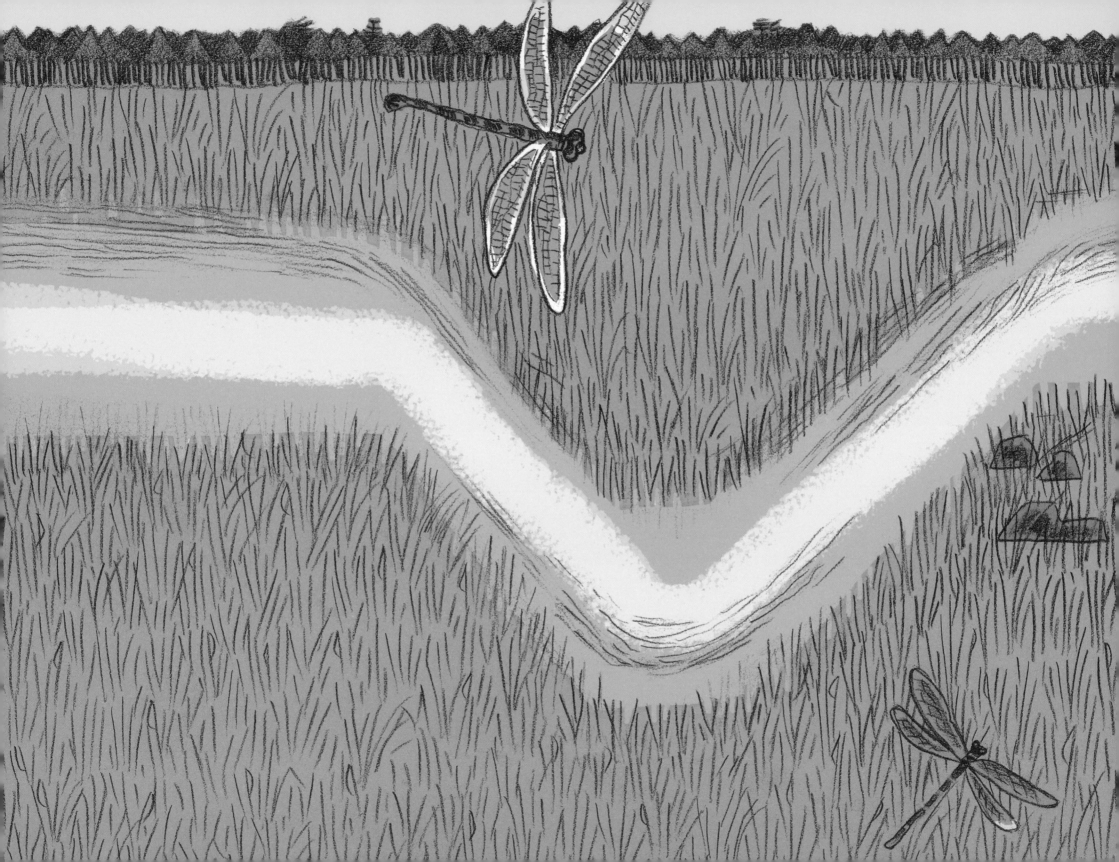

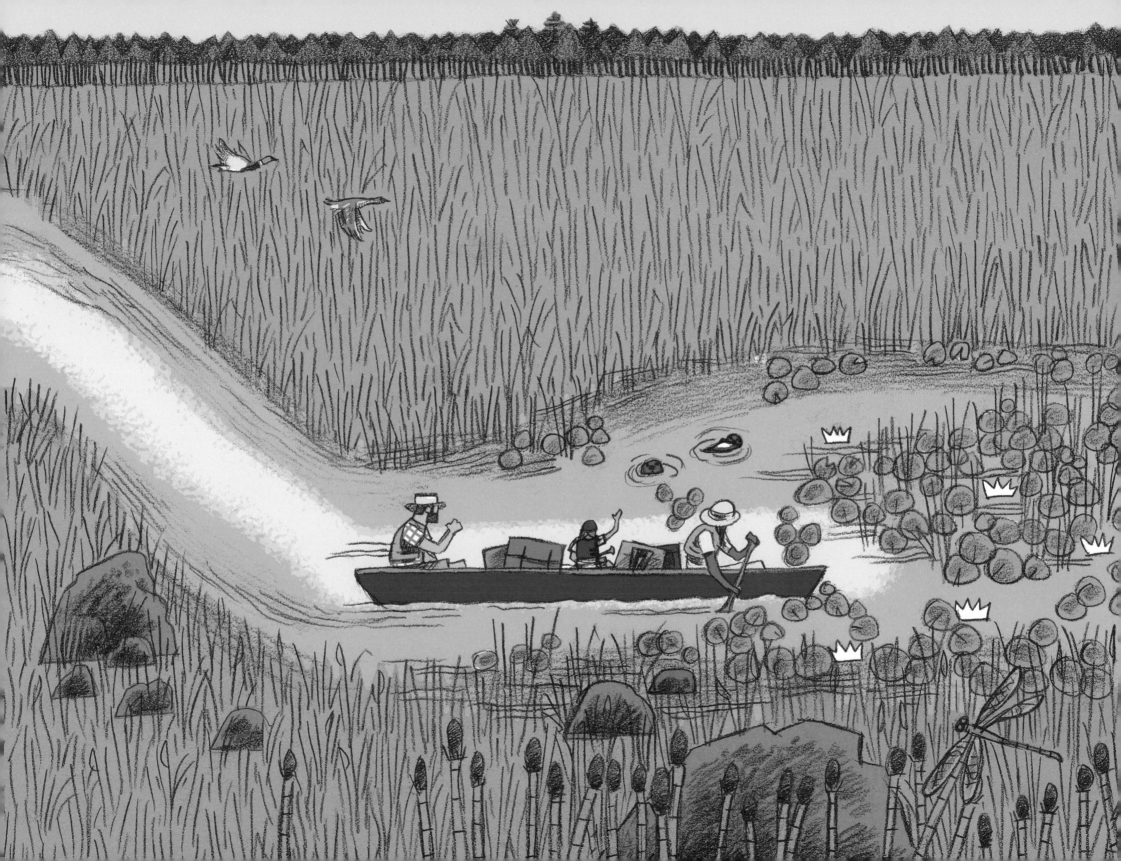

FOR STEVE AND CLIFF — J. O.

Exploration, discovery, and wonder: I've encountered each with every trip I have taken to the Boundary Waters Canoe Area Wilderness (commonly called the BWCA or BWCAW) in northern Minnesota. Visitors can paddle and portage a unique wilderness area that includes more than one thousand lakes and streams along the Canadian border. My experience canoeing, camping, hiking, and stargazing in the BWCAW was the inspiration for *One Summer Up North*. I hope every reader of this book might visit the BWCAW someday, and until then let the illustrations on these pages animate your imagination as you travel through the beautiful Boundary Waters Canoe Area Wilderness.

The University of Minnesota Press gratefully acknowledges the generous assistance provided for the publication of this book by the Margaret W. Harmon Fund.

Published by the University of Minnesota Press
111 Third Avenue South, Suite 290
Minneapolis, MN 55401-2520
http://www.upress.umn.edu

Artwork prepared for printing by color specialist Timothy Meegan

ISBN 978-1-5179-0950-5 (hc)
A Cataloging-in-Publication record for this title is available from the Library of Congress.

Printed in China on acid-free paper

The University of Minnesota is an equal-opportunity educator and employer.

25 24 23 22 21 20   10 9 8 7 6 5 4 3 2 1